Chronicles of Dragon Lore

T0148237

By
Julie A. Dickson

Chronicles of Dragon Lore

Written by Julie A. Dickson
Illustrated by Robin A. Morini

Order this book online at www.trafford.com
or email orders@trafford.com

Most Trafford titles are also available at major online book retailers.

Author Credits: Illustrations by Robin A. Morini Poems: The Invitation, Dragon Love,
Moethe's Fairy Dream by Robin A. Morini Poem: Dragon Lore by Julie A. Dickson

Printed in the United States of America.

ISBN: 978-1-4269-6694-1 (sc)
ISBN: 978-1-4269-6695-8 (e)

Trafford rev. 04/21/2011

 www.trafford.com

North America & international
toll-free: 1 888 232 4444 (USA & Canada)
phone: 250 383 6864 ♦ fax: 812 355 4082

Dedication

~To Sarah Beth and Matt~
Always follow your dreams

No More Destruction

Chronicles of Dragon Lore I

Ragethe the Scribe

Ragethe woke still holding the quill.
Ahh, he had fallen asleep while scribing the journal again…He yawned, a small burst of steam escaping his lips.

He heard Moethe in the outer chamber and wondered if she had eaten. He reveled at the idea of hunting with Moethe, her wings spread widely, glistening in the sun. Moethe was a beautiful green iridescent dragon with whirling silvery eyes, full of excitement at the prospect of a fresh kill.

Returning his thoughts back to the journal before him, he read what he had written the night before:

This account, written in the fourth millennium, reign of the Great Dragon Hycethe, follows the demise of the evil dragon Kenethe.

We have seen other species come into our realm. The coming together of minds has not kept the secrets of our kind, nor has it given us cause to neglect our primary focus. Peace.

I recall times past, when Dragons were killed mercilessly, our children slaughtered, during a time when the humans demanded our land and hunting grounds.

Our colony leader Rowethe was killed before our eyes, our kind left floundering until reunited by Hycethe.

We do not seek to destroy humans, but they have insisted on this adversarial pose, drawing weapons against us.

It is unseemly not to defend ourselves, yet I recall the slaughter and I wonder what is right to do... There remains the dragon code.

My own son Darethe was killed in the last battle of that reign. I am a mature dragon, resigned to being a scribe, living out the remainder of my years with Moethe.
Moethe sometimes forgets her sadness when we are hunting, and yet...

Moethe entered the chamber and looked anxiously at Ragethe. "Does Ragethe wish to hunt today?" she asked hopefully.

Ragethe smiled at Moethe, "Of course, my dear" as he closed the journal. His dark gray eyes looked lovingly at his mate, admiring her bright green scales, glimmering in the candlelight of the chamber.

Ragethe and Moethe leapt off the ledge of the cave and into the cool evening air to hunt.

Later that night, while Moethe slept peacefully on her ledge, Ragethe sitting at his journal, he gazed at her briefly before going back to his scribing.

Ragethe gathered his thoughts...he decided that he must recount the whole of dragon lore as he recalled it. His son was gone, this was truth, but how could what he knew disappear without being chronicled for those who came later? He was a scribe, after all. He began to write again.

A young dragon flew in the realm, young and perhaps not nearly as wise as the elders, this dragon called Ragethe, named by his mother Clarethe. When Ragethe emerged from the egg in the old days, his was the last and largest egg to hatch that day.

I recalled the stories of my mother as told to me...
Clarethe settled onto her haunches, proud to bear a son at last. She had two daughters, who would bear more dragons, but the dragon stock needed replenishing and she hoped that Ragethe would be a strong male. In the past, Clarethe had not been lucky enough to have a son live. In fact, this lot might be her only successful hatch. She recalled with horror of the time when the evil Kenethe sought out her nest of un-hatched children. She shook off the terrible

vision of this, knowing that previous sons were killed without the chance to see light.

Her mate, Banethe had tried to defend her, and flew at Kenethe, attacking him with talons and teeth. Clarethe had never seen such anger from her mate, not in battle, not in the hunt, but here he was risking his life and hers to attack Kenethe.

Banethe soon fell away from the larger Kenethe, wounded almost mortally that day, and hence, Clarethe and Banethe left the region for him to heal.

It was away in the land of mist that this laying of eggs took place, away from those who were loyal to Kenethe. Banethe lived long enough to see his son Ragethe and not much longer.

My father, Banethe's dying words to me were simple, "Ragethe, you must protect your mother and sisters when you are grown. Your mother has a hidden place to teach you what you must know. Choose your loyalty wisely, for know that I did not.

I foolishly believed that Kenethe was a good leader, but look what he has done... My son, you are the best hope for the future of dragon-kind. You must venture forth in time, seeking others, honorable in nature, for there are those who are not. How will you discover them, you might wonder? Look to the eyes, my son, for they tell all.

The other way of truth is to trust the faeries, for they are also ancients and know the ways of good and evil. There are those who would use the faeries for misdoings, and you must never stoop so low. "

And with his dying breath, Banethe, my father called my mother to him to say their goodbyes. I never really knew Banethe well, but in time I understood the lore from my mother's tongue, as I with my sisters, Jolethe and Lorethe sat in the moonlight listening on many a dark evening after my mother took us hunting.

My mother's words surrounding us, in the warmth of our hidden glen, firelight flickering in her eyes as she recounted the lore to us... "Banethe and I would often come across faeries in the realm and talk of dragon-lore. We trusted them, and as such, they knew many things of dragon-kind, as we do of faeries.

They are small ancients, magical in properties, flitting about amongst humans unnoticed. They often brought word of human-kind to dragons and forest-folk alike, and it is through faeries that we learned of trickery and deceit.

The forest-folk in their land often call the faeries in the moonlight, as they love the stories. Forest-folk are gatherers, a peaceful folk, perhaps human, but none are aware of what nature of being they are exactly. They are smaller than human, larger than faeries. Forest folk have no magical properties and do not live long in their lives.
They dwell in the wooded areas, and dragons have nothing to fear from them.

In calling the faeries with herbs in their lantern, in front of firelight, with such words that would entice them to come forth, they hear all. Often the dragons are called upon to tell of dragon-lore as has always been our custom, to provide some assurance of our continuation…in the telling.

The faeries would come, the panacea of many beasts, and they would entice dragons to share the stories. Unbeknownst to us, and perhaps even to them, for I would not place blame where none is due, stories of untruths were placed into the thoughts of faeries by the evil dragon Kenethe.

He called upon the faeries as many had, and what he told them was not to be heard of by humankind. What transpired hence was tragedy, Kenethe having used treachery on the faeries without their knowledge. He called upon magic to enchant a group of faeries during the telling. These faeries went to humans in sleep, whispering the secrets and untruths of dragon-lore into the ears of them, causing a vast chaos in our world.

From long ago, when humans first appeared to us, we thought them to be harmless, short in life-span, and dismissed them to their existence as unimportant. After this incident with Kenethe telling the faeries grave untruths of dragons, the humans came to believe that dragons were cruel and terrible beasts, who would rob them of their possessions, burn out their dwellings, kill them in their sleep, and capture their children!

What Kenethe did had dire consequences, and no dragons could fathom the purpose of these falsehoods being told to humans. Faeries, after the enchantment diminished, came sheepishly to trusted dragons and told all that had occurred. Almost paralyzed with anguish, since faeries and dragons have lived in harmony in this realm from the ancient times, the faeries swore not to share dragon-lore with humans again.

Even then, the dragons did not disparage the good name of faeries, knowing of the enchantment and treachery of Kenethe. Banethe and other dragons, now estranged from the evil Kenethe met with faeries and dismissed them of any wrongdoing.

The faeries then did swear to aid the dragons in learning of Kenethe's plans, but Kenethe had his spies among dragon-folk, and no such assistance was possible. Kenethe did the unthinkable after the incident, by dismissing his faerie-friend, Bluebell, after all attempts at poisoning her failed. [Faeries are not beings that are susceptible to death by poison]

And so the stories went, told to Ragethe, to me, the hidden son of Clarethe and Banethe. We lived in secrecy, leaving our misty valley only to hunt, and only when my mother had sought to leave the ledge, eyes widely looking for dangers, that her three children might live.

Jolethe and Lorethe were my only companions, save my mother, for two years. A dragon reaches early maturity in that time, but without dragon-kind around us, my mother still acted as protector. Soon, the hunting became difficult, and we ventured further and further from our valley, seeking food. On a cold evening in winter, we flew in silence, as Clarethe had taught us; I saw in the distance the spread wings of a powerful bronze dragon. I knew my mother saw as well, so I did not speak, although she exchanged glances with me. It was a silent signal to take my sisters into the glen below, quickly, in case he was hostile.

Jolethe and Lorethe followed me without question and we landed below. Jolethe was a blue dragon [like Clarethe] and Lorethe a green, while I was a dark gray dragon with silvery scales that glistened in the moonlight. I knew to hide us well, to cover our colors in the hogswort hedges and heavy thistle-brush in the glen.

I hoped that my mother fared well above, and I admit that it was one time I feared for my life, knowing that I was my sisters' protector and would have to defend them if it came to that. Since we were raised by my mother alone, we all had great respect for each other and got along well.
It was always understood that my sisters would follow my direction, if something happened to my mother.

Clarethe returned after a time, with the bronze dragon. As he landed, I recalled the words of my father, and gazed into his eyes, searching for the honesty or evil that my father had described to me as a hatchling. Clarethe spoke to us, and bowed slightly. "This is Rowethe, my children. He is the leader of the northern colony and has agreed that we may join them."

Following my mother's example, we all bowed slightly toward Rowethe, who was a magnificent bronze dragon with dark eyes.
I saw no evil in those eyes, at least none that I could discern in my small experience with these things. Rowethe spoke in a deep voice and we listened intently, for we had not heard such a voice since the death of my father.

"You are welcome, dragon-folk." He motioned behind him. "It is best that we go now, under cover of night, as our colony is well-hidden from enemies of the land. You must be quiet and ever vigilant when hunting or entering the colony, since we have suffered hard in our losses and there are many young to protect to adulthood that we might continue. Come now..." and he rose to his full height before taking off.

Clarethe, my sisters and I followed Rowethe through the night, and that marked the beginning of our new lives. We found fellow dragons in hiding, other strong children protected by fierce mothers. There were a few young males, but mostly females in this land, since the evil Kenethe had killed so many male offspring.

Rowethe often regaled us with stories of battle and warned us seriously of the dangers outside our world. "I cannot express the importance enough that we survive here. Ragethe, you are amongst the newest of the young males and will train with me when I give battle lessons."
He nodded to the section of young males, and they acknowledged me. I knew then, that my friendship and camaraderie with these peers was struck.

I was to learn what it took to be a battle dragon, as my father had. That night was the last night that my mother ever referred to me as one of her children. She sheparded my sisters around, showing them the ways of eggs, birth and hatchlings, knowing there was much to teach.

I knew something of female dragons, since I lived only with Clarethe and my sisters for two years, yet this new experience of the colony was overwhelming to me. There was the hunt, but at times, it felt as though I had no time to myself to think. My sisters often spoke of potential mates and eventually I told Clarethe that I would move to the male quarters with my fellow battle dragons-in-training.

My lessons with Rowethe were both terrifying and exciting. We hunted, practiced battle plans and fought each other playfully all of our days, and time passed. The other dragons accepted me, since Rowethe did, without question. I was becoming a large, imposing dragon, as Banethe had been in stature. Many of the others had been long established friends, from being together since they were hatchlings, but I mostly had Rowethe.

He eventually pushed me into a small group of males, the team leader being Balethe, an older dragon, who took me on as his practice partner. The other two in Balethe's team were Karethe and Kalethe, who were brothers and always remained skeptical of my existence there in the colony. I found out later that their own brother, who had been Balethe's previous partner, had died of a practice battle wound some time ago, and I felt sorrow for their loss.

Each team consisted of an older dragon, more experienced in battle, and several young dragons in training. Our team often served as a subject for Rowethe's lessons, as he spoke of lunging and flying at other dragons. We could only imagine such games in reality, since none of us had seen battle.

I knew of my father's deadly encounter with Kenethe, so I knew that the preparation for battle was necessary. But I was a dragon of great thinking and never wanted to see a battle. Even then, I might have felt more at ease scribing than fighting, but that was not to come until much later in my life.

I soon knew that my mother Clarethe was mated to Rowethe, and for the first time since my father's death, I felt instinctively that she had only survived his death for the purpose of protecting my sisters and me. Now she could let others teach and protect alongside her. She was a member of the colony, and the other females respected her.

One evening in summer, when the air was warm and the sounds carried, I heard voices from outside the glen. I spoke to Rowethe, and he told me that they were the voices of the forest-folk that I could hear, calling the faeries. I had often heard of faeries, and since both Banethe and Clarethe had spoken of them, I asked Rowethe whether I would be permitted to see them.

"Ragethe, we shall go together when the moon comes up...but understand that faeries, in their very nature are story-tellers. They want to hear the dragon-lore, but we risk discovery in the telling. We must protect our colony at all costs. Faeries will repeat the stories throughout the large land, and we cannot let ourselves be betrayed, even with the temptation of story-telling, which is great."

I assured Rowethe that I would not speak, and that even if I had wanted to, I had no stories to tell to the faeries. We entered into the glen where the forest-folk sat, and heard their words...

> "Out in the fields where the wild thyme grows,
> We sit under the moon glistening, full as the campfire soars
> A handful of thyme, a fistful of rosemary,
> Scented smoke spiraling upward to the midnight sky
> First calling the faeries, come one, come all
> Come dance and sing this enchanted eve"

I soon saw faeries begin to appear, ever shimmery in their appearance; I was intrigued but not fearful, since I stood with Rowethe in the shadows, unseen. When the faeries settled at the campfire, the forest-folk spoke again:

> "To the fire then throw two fistfuls of Ocimum Basilicum
> And call the dragons forth..."

And then the faeries began to dance and chant....

> **"Calling all dragons, calling you near**
> **The fire is calling, calling you here**
> **We're not afraid, old dragons of yore**
> **Inviting you here to share dragon lore."**

So this was the invitation that Rowethe spoke of.

We ventured forward to the fire, Rowethe before me. The vast size of Rowethe did overwhelm the forest-folk, who cringed in fear, until he told them he meant no harm to them. Into the night, Rowethe told his stories of times past, and I was aware that never once, did he disclose the location of his colony.

I felt safe there, the heat of the fire was soothing, and for a time I felt lost in the lore, as if it was my own father again speaking to me. I blinked, realizing that Rowethe had become both father and teacher to me, and for that I was grateful.

When I met the faeries, I must admit my surprise at how forward they were, touching my limbs and head, as if they already knew me.

Rowethe explained that faerie touch was healing and enchanting to dragons and that it was an honor to be chosen for faerie touch. The faeries spoke in soft tones; in fact at times I had to strain to hear them speak.

They sat on small rocks amongst the forest-folk, whom I noticed were in great awe of the faeries and beckoned them to ask us our dragon-lore. "Speak to us, great Rowethe of your lore. Who is this young one, this gray, handsome dragon with the glistening eyes?" a faerie in a filmy garment of blue asked, touching Roweth's face as he listened to her.

I learned their names after a time, and that faeries had the names of flowering plants. They explained that it guarded them against evil, since anyone speaking their names might only be mentioning the plants around them. The one in blue seemed to be Iris, while others were Dianthus, Rose and Hyacinth. They explained that faeries were ancient and whimsical creatures that often appeared and disappeared at will.

Faeries had since times past, been friends and cohabitants of the land with dragons, even in a time when neither could recall the existence of forest-folk or humans. Some dragons and each leader dragon had a personal faerie, a friend who kept close to him and brought news.

Faeries each wore an amulet of soft cloth, and I wondered at the purpose of these. Dianthus explained that amulets were within the faerie belief of healing and protection.
They often gathered special herbs, plants and flowers for healing, and even dragon blood, from the battle ground of slain dragons to become part of the amulet. Each kept a flower of her name in the amulet, denoting their connection to the earth, and apparently they held some faith of earth worship that I was unaware of. I knew only from Banethe and my mother that faeries were

long-lived beings, magical and mystical. Thus, I was intrigued to know what properties and customs faeries had.

It was then that I noticed the amulets around the necks of the forest-folk, and decided that the faeries had passed this custom to them for the purpose of protection.

Alas, the forest-folk had such a need, since they were a vulnerable creature. During these stories, the forest-folk only listened and nodded, obviously having great respect for faeries. I did not know if the forest-folk were related to humans or of a different species and no information was told to me on this. I understood the forest-folk to be smaller in stature and that they lived simply in hollowed out trees, while humans seemed to dwell in great castles built by their own hands.

Iris spoke in apparent embarrassment of the time when Kenethe had deceived them, and touched Rowethe all the more, seemingly to show their kindness and loyalty to dragon-kind. They offered to make amulets for Rowethe and for me, but Rowethe declined, that they would inhibit flight. I would have liked a faerie amulet, but said nothing after Rowethe declined.

I was still a young dragon and took my lead from Rowethe. I learned much that night, of the history of our kind, from Rowethe's words. I realized that even though I was told stories constantly by my mother, that it was but a snippet of dragon-lore, and I longed to know as much as I could.

I now better understood the uncertainty that dragons faced. Humans were perhaps our biggest enemy, as they often killed without cause, and we had been powerless to retaliate, due to dragon code, we did not kill any species except to hunt.

Dragons were forced at times, to choose between their code and their own survival, but there were those who believed that dragons who had broken the code of killing were ones who became evil. Such was the belief that the fate of Kenethe had come about in this manner.

Rowethe spoke of great castles and humans with armor who feared dragons and actually sought them out. Usually, dragons had avoided contact with humans, but these knights on their horse-creatures now rode into the dragon colonies and killed them in daylight, some hatchlings even as they slept.

I felt fortunate to not have seen humans and wondered more of their existence and how such a vulnerable creature could pose such a threat to dragon-kind.

And then was told the story of Kenethe, who had been away on a hunt for several days. The sight of his slain colony facing him upon his return was so devastating that he flew in rage to the castle and took part in a vast slaughter of humans, along with many other battle dragons who followed him. Some dragons fell with arrows piercing them dead on the ground, and others lay with mortal wounds, awaiting death. Kenethe fled finally, with his remaining battle dragons behind him, and his reign of terror followed.

When Kenethe acted in deceit, having broken dragon-code, he amplified the problem we faced with humans. Instead of resolving the conflict, humans would now pose a much greater threat to dragons. Rather than inhabiting large glens, basking in the sun, raising their young and avoiding humans, dragons were destined to hide from them that our species would survive and recover from the slaughter.

Dragons do not reproduce in quantity, and many offspring do not survive, making the colony very important to guard and keep secret.

Kenethe had not only broken dragon code, but tricked the faeries into helping him lure the humans into further confrontations. Some loyal dragons thought Kenethe's actions were warranted, considering the human invasion upon his colony, but in times hence, he had lost his senses and turned against his own kind as well. His prosperity and that of his own offspring, he believed, depended upon the killing of the male dragon offspring of dragons that would oppose him.

And such was my personal history, the death of my mother's children and the death of my father, Banethe...who had once been one of Kenethe's own battle dragons, having fought alongside him.

I understood more about Kenethe now, and the pain and loss that must have provoked him into killing humans. Still, I felt that the dragon-code was strong, and wondered if many dragons would have chosen his path.

Rowethe and I left the scene, with me quiet and thinking. Finally Rowethe, sensing my uncertainty and confusion about all that I had heard, spoke to me as we soared to the hunt.

"Ragethe, I want you to know that Banethe was a brave and honorable dragon. He never became the evil dragon that Kenethe is now. Kenethe does not have the respect of dragons, as he would presume from his battles with humans. No, we are in fact, ashamed to be thought of this way. I long for days to return to peace, in such a time when dragons might live without chaos and battle.

I fear that another battle looms in the future, a final battle for me, that I might defeat Kenethe and end the reign of evil that he has aspired to."

I looked at Rowethe and as much as I wanted to respond, I had no words that seemed fitting. He was a good colony leader, and I had much admiration and respect for him. He had confided to me that he might defeat Kenethe, but I felt that he was risking himself and our whole colony in doing so, yet I said nothing.

I looked over at the sleeping Moethe, recalling the day we were mated. She slept gracefully, as she did all things. The vision of her vast wing-span and elegant swooping movements never ceased to amaze me. My love for Moethe was endless. I only wished that Moethe could have had a son that lived. Our daughters were wonderful females, with many children and Moethe took great pleasure in watching them.
I could always see in Moethe's eyes, when she was thinking of Darethe, our only son…. I turned back to my writing.

During the time when my mother brought my sisters and me to Rowethe's colony, I came of age, and of course my mother set about the task of finding me a suitable mate. After many females were introduced to me, I found that there was only one that I noticed. Her name was Moethe. When I told my mother my choice, she hesitated only briefly, and then arranged the meeting. We were to be mated! The night approached and I waited for Moethe in my chamber.

Moethe entered:

> The mist arose from around her,
> reminding me of the ancient past
> and a future yet unknown.
> The mist rose…gently swirling,
> her scent touching me,
> her oiled, perfumed skin
> arousing my senses…

She spoke:

> "My beloved, my heart's desire
> I've come to your abode"

As I stood there to welcome my love in the dragon's mist.
Her majestic presence enveloped me, as the mists warmly heated the air.

I answered her:

> "Come in, my love, come in..."

My Moethe... That was how I always thought of her. And when our son was hatched, we watched him in awe as he emerged from his egg. "Darethe" Moethe whispered, "His name is Darethe". I nodded.

Darethe grew quickly in the colony, trained with the males at an early age. After two years, he was soaring in battle practice with the rest of us.

I saw the concern in my Moethe's eyes, as Rowethe spoke of the eventual confrontation with Kenethe, or 'Evil Kenethe' as most of us referred to him.

Our daughters Corethe and Clinethe grew as Darethe did, and my Moethe took them in hand as my mother once had for my sisters. Jolethe and Lorethe had prospered and given birth to young dragons, as Moethe and I had. They hovered around the hatchlings, with Clarethe looking on, recalling her own responsibilities from the past. Clarethe spent her days, well-earned, sunning herself and looking forward to hunting with Rowethe. Our colony was very close and all of us were loyal to Rowethe.

Now and then we heard of other colonies, when a visiting dragon wandered into our glen, but mostly we stayed hidden, awaiting Rowethe's prophecy that he would have to face Kenethe. He continued training us, so that we might fly beside him, well prepared for the battle.

One day, word reached us that Kenethe had laid waste to another castle, and when we went to see, the remnants were still smoldering. Not a stone was left standing. What hadn't been destroyed by fire had been rampaged by Kenethe and his battle dragons. No sign of life remained, and I found myself wondering whether the humans had escaped this attack, or whether Kenethe had destroyed them with the castle.

We were angered and outraged that such devastation occurred, another violation of our dragon code. We all looked at Rowethe who bellowed, raised his head to the sky and roared, as if in agony "No more destruction! Kenethe has broken dragon code for long enough, and now I will break code to destroy him..."

Balethe, my partner and I looked at each other. Rowethe was not yet giving us battle instructions and we awaited his signal, as did the others. We were trained not to question Rowethe, and even if we questioned his words, it was not our place to argue with our colony leader.

We all watched Rowethe as he rose to the sky, full wings spanning, head tossing in anger. We knew that this was the final confrontation we had feared would come. I wished I had known the consequences of the following scene. Had I sensed the immediate danger to my only son, I might have sent him home, but no...even had I wished it, Darethe was raised for battle, as was I. We were stronger together, and together we flew.

The dragons were silent in following Rowethe, our leader, though we knew not what was coming, for certain. Most of us were trained battle dragons, yet untried in real battle. We were alert, eyes fixed upon both Rowethe and the ground below, seeking our adversary.

We met Kenethe alone in front of an abandoned castle, where he gloated his last victory, coiled up in anticipation of our arrival. "What's this?" Kenethe roared at us. "I am the Great Dragon Leader, how dare you challenge me?"

Rowethe hesitated not, as he soared toward Kenethe with terrifying speed. Kenethe struck Rowethe down with flame and teeth, and to the shock of many of us, Rowethe was dead. The vast amount of killing must have made Kenethe strong and confident. Our colony leader killed before our eyes and seething with anger, the rest of us flew at Kenethe, hoping to overpower him with our numbers.

Darethe fell soon after and all I could think of was my Moethe and how she would grieve for him. The battle dragons fought gallantly and finally, three older dragons joined force and put an end to Kenethe's reign of fear and destruction. His broken body lay before the castle, left as a reminder of all the killing and sorrow he had caused.

I stood on the ground before Darethe's body, my son, dead. I looked into his dragon's eye, as was our custom and said my goodbye privately, as my fellow battle dragons allowed me some time to mourn his passing. The dragon custom was to be with a passing dragon, to look into his eye as the departing soul was released into the universe. Some dragons died alone, and I was never certain of what happened to their souls.

I regretted not bringing Darethe back to his mother, my Moethe. She was so skeptical of his passing I had all I could do to convince her that her son was gone. She asked my fellows to confirm Darethe's death, and they recounted the story of the battle to her. She quietly listened and then went into our chamber alone. I wanted to follow, to comfort her, but I had no words. I spent the night on the ledge outside our chamber, hearing her almost silent sobs from without.

In the morning, my sisters came to tell me that Clarethe was dead. She was so saddened by the news of Rowethe's death, that she, herself faded away in the night.
I had lost so much in one day I could hardly bear the pain inside of me.

My mother, Clarethe, was gone. Her mate and my teacher Rowethe, struck down in battle. I was consoled only by the knowledge that Kenethe was dead. I wished that I could have been the one to avenge my father's death, in killing Kenethe, but it was not to be so. And then my only son, Darethe was killed, in the same battle. I looked into the chamber to Moethe.

She was very still, and I approached her slowly, not knowing whether she wanted me near. She looked at me, her eyes shiny with dragon tears and asked, "Why?" I simply shook my head and held her. After a time, she spoke to me. "Ragethe, dear Ragethe, we must leave this place. There is too much death here. I can't bear it another moment. Please take me away."

And we left. Moethe and I left the colony and found our way south, to an unknown land where we seldom saw dragons. For many years, all I heard from passing dragons was of the senseless slaughter of our kind.

Humans were seeking our lands and our hunting grounds. I incorrectly thought that with Kenethe's death that the killing would cease, but some things take a long time to change.

Moethe and I for a long time saw our daughters Corethe and Clinethe as our only visitors. Their presence was often of some comfort to my Moethe, but more often than not, she preferred the solitude of our chamber in the south. Moethe and I had a quiet existence, one that I had dreamed of in my youth, long before the thought of battle ever loomed. The dragon-lore was something that was passed dragon-to-dragon, and sometimes through faeries, but seldom had any dragon scribed.

Sometime ago, I had heard of the new Great Dragon leader, Hycethe who was coming into power and leading all of dragon-kind into a new era of peace. I ventured out and approached Hycethe, looking into his eyes in the way my father Banethe taught me. I saw only honesty there, and decided that I would be loyal to him.

We had many meetings, what he called the meeting of the minds, when we planned and organized our thoughts for the future. It was then that the task of scribing dragon-lore was set upon me by Hycethe, which I accepted.

I had always felt that a record of lore would be an interesting way to chronicle dragons. The constant story-telling by dragons and the re-telling by faeries only served to change the content, and while entertaining, Hycethe agreed that an accurate version would be useful. Scribing was something that Hycethe had learned of from his experiences, and hence my Chronicle began.

Hycethe was unique in such a way that I have not known of any other dragon. Hycethe was acquainted with a human.

This unusual acquaintance came about in such an accidental way, that Hycethe in his wisdom saw the opportunity to change the future of both humans and dragons. In his realm, Hycethe had come across an injured human. He might not have approached the human, however, he appeared to be dead and Hycethe was naturally curious, never having seen a human up close. It happened that the human was only sleeping, and awoke suddenly when Hycethe leaned over him. Having no weapon in hand, the human gasped and closed his eyes in fear, thinking that the massive dragon above would kill him. Instead, Hycethe brought the human food and water and attempted to converse with him.

The human was a princely being, called Anslem, having been felled by his horse and he was healing there. The horse was also apprehensive about Hycethe at first, until Anslem quieted him. Once Anslem knew that Hycethe would not harm him, he was actually as curious about dragons as Hycethe was about humans.

Hycethe saw his opportunity, using Anslem's injury to stay with him and find out more about humans. Hycethe and Anslem spent many days and nights in conversation each learning about the other and their kind.

Hycethe developed an understanding of humans, although he thought of them as forest-folk, rather fragile and short lived beings. He explained to Anslem that dragons could live a long time, and if not for battle, often lived close to 1000 years. Anslem told Hycethe about the structure of the castles, humans and why humans were so innately mistrustful of dragons. Apparently they feared large beasts, even if they were not attacked by them, and the philosophy of humans was to kill what they feared.

Hycethe nodded in understanding to Anslem, although he told him that unlike humans, dragons killed only in the hunt. It was hard for Anslem to accept the idea at first, that dragons did not find importance in having territory or taking land. Hycethe assured him that they often relocated to better hunting grounds, but it sounded to Hycethe that land possession and material substances were human traits, not shared by dragons.

In this manner, a new type of friendship was forged between Anslem and Hycethe. Anslem related the custom of scribing to Hycethe and he was both intrigued and interested, that dragon-lore be recorded. Anslem told Hycethe that many generations of humans relied on their records to teach crafts, to records births and deaths, and keep accurate accounts of trade and custom.

Anslem returned to the humans and spoke to them of dragons. Hycethe took his story of humans back to his dragon colony, and henceforth Hycethe began to think of the future as having the possibility of peace. He and Anslem made a pact to meet again, and Anslem thought that he could persuade the humans to cease the attacks upon the dragon colonies. Not battling humans was something that Hycethe as a peace-loving dragon, wanted to pursue, and he vowed to forge this new peace.

When Hycethe told me of human scribing, providing me with the book Anslem gave to him, I felt that I had always been meant to scribe dragon-lore, having thought of this for a long time. Now that so many years have passed in the millennium, I look back on my scribing and wonder at the multitude of time I have devoted.

When I chronicled my beginnings, I felt that it substantiated my existence somehow.

When I read of Darethe and the battle to my Moethe, she relived it from my perspective. In my meetings with Hycethe, he assures me that his quest for peace with the humans, with Anslem's help, may actually become a reality. I believe that my Chronicle will serve to preserve the dragon-lore and help us to relate to humans.

I can only hope that Hycethe's dream for peace happens in my lifetime, or at least in the future, for my sister's children and my daughters and their children.

I closed the journal for the evening and went to lie beside my Moethe, who was still asleep. I admired her as much as the day we mated and yet so many years have passed now. I closed my eyes and dreamed of far away places, with no death and only happiness, where I could be with Moethe, my love.

I felt Moethe stir beside me, and knew that, she was deep inside her dreams. I hoped than in dreaming, Moethe found peace and a place far away from the pain she felt upon waking.

Moethe dreams a faerie dream:

> In a distant land
> I have not visited
> There grows a tree

With dragon history
[I have seen in my mind's eye]
This was a place where
Blood was spilt by
The mighty dragons
Seeping into the soil
The blood and earth did blend
Earth Mother has grown the
Dracaena Draco tree
Rich is the sap, reddish and brown
It is gathered by the faeries,
Collected and congealed
Into a hardened resin
The dragon's blood offers
The attributes of protection
To those who carry it
Within their amulets

Moethe awakened, thinking of Darethe, her lost son.
She wondered if the faeries had sent the dream to her, knowing of her sorrow.
Perhaps the blood of her son served them well, protecting the faeries.
Perhaps his death had not been totally in vain, if his blood served them.
Perhaps Darethe lived on……

HATCHLING

Chronicles Of Dragon Lore II

Dragon Beginnings

Hycethe and Ragethe were having one of their many meetings, after Hycethe enlisted Ragethe to scribe the dragon-lore as a written history.

"This is a great task set before you, Ragethe. I trust that you are quite accurate in your scribing and will record our lore for all to read in generations to come. Too long have I remained silent. There are tales that I have not yet imparted to any dragon, stories of the past, the very beginnings of dragon kind", Hycethe explained.

Ragethe could barely contain his excitement, for even as he had scribed lore from his own lifetime, this is what he had awaited for so long. The times of the first millennium, of which he knew almost nothing, but the occasional whisperings of the faeries.

Ragethe listened for hours, as Hycethe told him astonishing stories of dragon past millenniums. He found that Hycethe was perhaps one of the oldest dragons in existence now. With Kenethe dead, Hycethe was the great leader of the dragon realm.
He had colony leaders, as always, keeping in close contact with them, and Hycethe knew of all the lore of the ancient times.

Ragethe felt that Hycethe must be feeling his age and his own mortality, if he was so concerned about chronicling the early dragon lore.

Later that evening, Ragethe settled in for an evening of scribing, as was his custom after hunting with Moethe. He often scribed until just before dawn, when he joined Moethe in sleep.

In the beginning, the dragons lead a peaceful existence in the realm, knowing of no other presence of beings save the faeries. The dragons and faeries conversed regularly, faeries visiting the dragon colonies, witnessing births and often carrying news to other colonies. This little relationship was congenial, in that they offered each other friendship, perhaps help when it was required, but never interfered with each other.

Dragons by their nature were large beasts, though a variety of sizes and colorations existed. The females were generally brighter in color, in shades of blue and green. Males were larger than females and were usually black, grey, bronze, silver or gold. Hycethe was a gold dragon, while I, Ragethe am grey. Many dragons have whirling, shimmery eyes that shine in moonlight or firelight.

Dragons are able to breathe fire when desired, however the flame is reserved for certain times, such as for scorching a path in rough terrain. They used talon and teeth with prey, and never flame.
Dragon prey could range from fish in the blue sea, birds and rodents, to larger hoofed beasts that ran in herds. Prey might differ by region or by time of year. Dragons only killed during the hunt, and only what they could eat at the time.

Dragons were never known to fight one another, except in challenge for a mate on occasion. This type of fight was as it sounds, a challenge and never to the death. In the entire realm, there was one Great Dragon Leader.

Within each colony of dragons, there was a leader, his mate and many other, lesser dragons. The leader was never challenged, but when he died, the next dragon in line for leader was usually the eldest and strongest male. If a colony became too large, a lesser male dragon might take his family and others to start a new colony, but this was a natural occurrence.

Besides hunting, mating and teaching our offspring, dragons often devised playful games to teach agility. This aided in flight and in the hunt. Dragons could be very lazy beasts, basking and napping in afternoon sun, or dipping into the cool, blue sea on warm days.

They dwelled either in cave, in glen or in protected valley, depending upon which part of the realm a colony was located in.

A dragon's home was usually referred to as a chamber or perhaps a nest when eggs were present. Females matured at about two years of age, and a mate could be found. Eggs were laid, and females usually could hatch from 1-3 eggs in their first lay. Older females were known to have 6 eggs, but not all hatched, and not all hatchlings survived. The number of offspring depended solely upon the dragon population, as it was self-governing. Too many dragons might have trouble finding sufficient prey.

Dragons have a long lifespan, if there is sufficient food and they are not wounded, many live to be close to 1000 years. A five hundred year old dragon is still considered young. Older dragons always take responsibility for teaching the young. Since faeries live as long as dragons, they often share a long-term friendship, if a faerie takes a liking to one dragon.

During the first millennium one colony of dragons was located in the southern part of the realm, the leader being Noethe, who was a magnificent gold dragon, his colony large and peaceful. His mate, Marethe and he had been together for most of the millennium and their children prospered before them, producing many offspring.

They did not often venture to other colonies, but Noethe himself made the quest in spring before the warm days and prior to the coldest days of winter for the meeting of minds with the Great Dragon Leader, Dracethe.

Dracethe, a powerful and huge black dragon with dazzling green eyes had been leader for the entire millennium. If there was another prior to Dracethe, no dragon could recall…

Dracethe welcomed the colony leaders to this meeting with faeries leading them into the hidden glen. Dracethe was a great believer in staying united with the faeries, as they were long-ranged beings, who often brought word of flock and herd to the dragons, along with whispers of other lands.

It had always been so, that the Great Dragon Leader had held a meeting of the minds in this manner, and amongst them, any recent dragon-lore was exchanged. They proudly recounted births in their colonies, stories of the hunt and other dragon tales, to be carried back to colonies by the leaders.

It so happened that at the start of this meeting, the faeries were fluttering about them.

Dracethe soon became aware of unusual twitterings, which were not the custom of faeries. They seemed to want audience to share great news.

The faerie most well known to him hovered about by his left ear, begging to speak. "Dear Dracethe, we must be telling of the humans". Heather was his faerie-friend and was wearing a filmy green garment that billowed about so, that if Dracethe had not known she was there, he might have mistaken her for a cool autumn breeze.

Dracethe nodded, "All right Heather", [faeries always carried the name of plants] "What is your important news of 'humans'?" Dracethe wondered at the unfamiliar word.

Heather seemed to settle down a bit in his acceptance and the other faeries joined her on a fallen tree. They were Tulip, Gardenia and Daffodil by name, and all of the leader dragons knew them, from their visits to the colonies.

Heather spoke softly, "In the middle land, close to the great hill you have spoken of as Pale Mountain, we have witnessed the arrival of a being so unusual that we have watched them for a time before bringing word to you at this place."

The dragon leader Dracethe looked around at the colony leaders, to Noethe of the south, Kirethe of the north, Hanethe of the east and Hacethe of the west, and could tell by their expressions that they knew nothing of this news. "Please continue, Heather" Dracethe bade her.

Heather resumed her story, "It was at the beginning of warm days, when we first saw these humans, although we did not know what they were then. We went to them in shadows to hear them speak, and watched them erect large stone structures. We did not understand their intentions, yet soon we knew that they were being built as shelters. Dracethe, we knew not what they what the beings were, but they call themselves human.

We listened at the structure walls, and they talked so much that we learned much in a short while. They have mates and offspring, but they are frail and often fall to death or get something called disease. They have a special human called a wizard, who does magic to assist ailing humans, but the magic is not faerie-like, it is something else entirely!

We watched a wizard draw a potion from woodland plants and steep a strong odorous substance that the humans drank. He spoke words that were strange, and could only be as part of the magic, creating smoke of colors with odors." Dracethe asked, "And what of these humans? Do they hunt as we do? What manner of appearance do they have?"

Heather nodded nervously as if anticipating his questions, "They hunt the woodland beasts, but they put the carcasses to flame before they eat them. They often go through a ritual in the hunting area, leaving the entrails and heads behind, taking only the flesh and hide of the beasts. The remains are left to carrion birds and jackals. They somehow prepare the hides of animals they have killed to cover themselves. They are almost hairless beings, these humans. They are walking on two legs and are not very large in size."

"How odd", Dracethe remarked. "These humans are living in the realm and yet I have never seen one. I wonder what place they have arrived from."

"We discovered that humans can be enchanted by faerie song, so within our music we may slip in and out of their dwellings unseen. In listening to humans, we learned that they came over the blue sea in a vessel that they built of timbers, bringing objects with them there are made not of wood or stone. We touched the objects, not knowing their purpose and they were colder than stone in winter, but glimmering as the sea.

We saw them throw one such object at prey, the beast dropped and bled until they ran up to kill it with another smaller pointed object. Humans have no large teeth, nor talons, and they seem to kill prey using these objects", Heather explained.

Noethe spoke, "Great Leader Dracethe, it seems that these humans may stay in our realm, yet perhaps they know nothing of our existence. I wonder if we shall stay unknown to them until a time when the faeries can determine more of their nature. It is not disturbing that they are hunters, but what of these cold objects?"

Dracethe turned to all of the dragon leaders, "What the faeries speak of is something unknown to us. To act upon this without further knowledge or understanding would not be wise. I agree with Noethe, and wish all of you to remain hidden to these humans until the time of our next meeting.

I wish the faeries to visit me often with more word of the humans, to tell of their customs, that we might be prepared to communicate with them, since they have language. They may be an intelligent being and as such, could be worthy of our acquaintance. How say you all?"

All colony leaders murmured their agreement, and the meeting soon dissolved.

As promised, Heather and other faeries made many visits to Dracethe to tell of the humans and their customs.

Ragethe laid his quill down for the night, thinking that he must resume this journal writing soon. Many stories of dragon lore were floating in his head, and he longed to scribe them to parchment, yet his eyes were heavy.

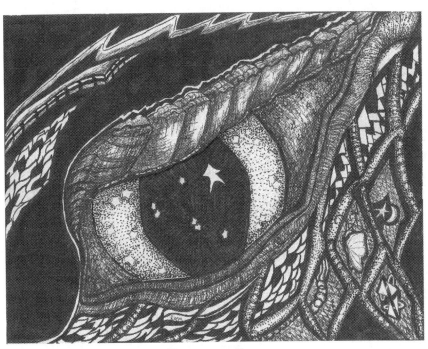

DRAGON EYE

Chronicles of Dragon Lore III

Dragon Code

Ragethe settled in with his quill and journal to scribe the history of dragons.

He looked over his last entries, and decided to scribe about how Dragon Code came to be. He recalled the day when Hycethe sadly told the tale of how everything in the peaceful dragon world changed with one incident.

Noethe was on his ledge in front of the chamber where his mate, Marethe was inside, when the faerie Star Flower approached. She flew in close to him and bade him greeting. He offered her some fresh goat's milk, knowing that it was her favorite, and invited her to speak. She often came to him to tell stories of what the faeries had learned of humans.

"Noethe, I have much to tell today", Star started slowly, as if not knowing where to begin. "Heather is with Dracethe as we speak and I presume to say that he will order a meeting of the dragon leaders. Something unexpected and terrible has happened."

Noethe looked at Star intensely, waiting for what news could be so terrible. He thought that it would be bad news, such as the death of a great dragon. "Tell me." He said.

"A human has been killed by a dragon." Star said simply.

"He wandered into the hunting grounds of a young male dragon called Barethe, to the east of the mountain. Barethe was after a herd, and somehow a human was crouching among them on the ground. When Barethe dove into the herd, the human was killed."

Noethe pondered this. "Was the human killed by accident, mistaken for prey?" He couldn't imagine a dragon seeking out a human at all, after Dracethe's previous order to remain unseen by humans.

"It was an accident. Barethe did not see the human. He may have been, in fact, hiding in the herd when he saw Barethe in the sky; the human was so low among the herd beasts." Star wrung her tiny hands.

"But the human was killed, and Barethe was distraught. Not knowing what to do, he fled to his colony leader, Hanethe to tell him of this unfortunate occurrence."

Noethe thought for a moment. "One human was killed by a dragon. This is a terrible thing to happen, especially after what Dracethe said, but...."

Star interrupted him, "But, Noethe, it doesn't end there".
"Barethe did not take the dead human away. He lay in the field with the herd beasts. And what Barethe did not see was that a group of humans witnessed the killing from the edge of the forest. What happened next was even more terrible."

Noethe's eyes whirled in anticipation. He impatiently said, "Honestly, Star, you take so long in the telling! Please finish the tale, if I must go to Dracethe soon!"

"Very well, Noethe." Star smoothed her garment, not wishing to anger her dragon friend. "Barethe returned to the field with Hanethe and the humans killed him."

"The humans killed Barethe?" Noethe asked.

"Not Barethe. They killed Hanethe." Star waited and watched Noethe.

Noethe stared at her. A leader had been killed? This unfortunate accident had quickly grown into a huge catastrophe and he knew that he must leave immediately to meet with Dracethe.

Noethe took off from the ledge, not even bidding farewell to Star. Noethe thought about the possible fate of dragons that this incident had occurred. What would Dracethe do?

Was any of Noethe's own colony in danger? Should he have waited and spoken to another dragon before he left? He shook off all of his questions and decided to wait for the meeting with Dracethe.

As Noethe arrived in the hidden glen, he saw that he was not the first. Many dragons had arrived and were awaiting Dracethe to address them.

"You have come quickly, my leaders." Dracethe turned to face each of them. "I know not the solution to this problem we face, but I have thought on it, and have devised the Dragon Code. Henceforth, the Dragon Code will be followed by all dragons. There are those who have promised revenge for the death of Hanethe. We must not act my fellow dragons! Barethe stands here before you, devastated by a terrible accident and what followed. He alone should have faced the humans, since he did the deed...but he is young. Sometimes we can forgive youth, but in this case, we were not given the chance to contemplate the misdeed, however accidental, before the humans brought death to Hanethe with their weapons."

Dracethe emphasized his position by standing tall and upright, turning with each phrase, that he might see the eyes of the other leaders.

Noethe spoke. "Great leader Dracethe, how will we make this right? Will the humans forget this accident, or is there danger to our mates and our young?"

Dracethe nodded slowly. "I fear that there is danger. Yes, the humans may now be hostile. When Barethe left the field a second time, he was seen by humans. They followed him partway to his colony. Barethe sounded a warning and the remainder of the colony fled the region immediately in haste. I believe the entire colony would have been at risk, had Barethe not warned them. This does not excuse Barethe for the misdeed, be certain. These humans, I am told by Heather, are a vindictive sort. They may seek out dragons, now that they know of our existence and one of their own has been killed. I want the emphasis clear. No killing of humans. This is the Dragon Code. We will avoid conflict with humans, and hope that no further incidents occur. If colonies have to be moved to avoid contact, then so be it."

The leader dragons all nodded in agreement. They left the meeting with the new Dragon Code in place, and returned to their colonies. The ones closest to the human region decided to move further away. For many years, the Dragon Code was followed.

Ragethe paused in thought, realizing that the incidents in his own lifetime might not have occurred if this original accident had not happened. He felt sorrow for Barethe, since he never intended harm to a human, and certainly not to his leader, Hanethe. How terrible for a leader to die that way! He returned to his scribing, knowing that he needed to finish this tale before he slept.

In the second millennium, once the great dragon Dracethe had passed in his old age, Noethe took over leadership of the dragon realm. Noethe had memories of Dracethe and kept the traditions with the two meetings in spring and autumn. He allowed the leaders audience to speak their thoughts, and not very much changed in the second millennium.

There were more unfortunate attacks by humans on dragon colonies. The losses were grave, but the dragon code was not breached. The colonies were attacked in daylight, as dragons basked and napped in the sun. They were taken by the same weapons as before, and the dragons learned to hide themselves more carefully, realizing that the humans were venturing further into the realm.

New structures were built by humans, and Noethe knew of many human settlements across the realm. Soon, something would have to be done.

He sought out Star Flower, his faerie friend to report on human activity when she could, understanding that humans were hostile to dragons, and there would always be danger to them.

Ragethe laid his quill down for the night, and went to rest. He was both invigorated and saddened by his task of recording dragon lore. The history of the realm was not all happiness. There was much sadness, but as a wise dragon, he knew that dragons had been sharing the realm with other creatures for perhaps three millennium. Most of the beings co-existed without conflict, and he hoped again that Hycethe's plan for the future could mean a new peace, and not a future wrought with pain and killing, such as the lore that he was scribing from the past. Oh, to be in a time when there was no threat of killing. Not to live in fear, not to battle dragons, or to worry about humans. Ragethe fell asleep with that thought in his head....

FOREST FOLK

Chronicles of Dragon Lore IV

Emergence of Forest Folk

Ragethe decided that he had not yet scribed any tales on the emergence of the forest-folk, the simple beings living in the forest. He began to write…..

It was the custom of the faeries to visit the dragon leaders and especially the great dragon leader, Noethe. Noethe's liaison with the faeries was called Star Flower, a fluttery blue-clad faerie who arrived almost unseen, to settle into the air near his ear, whispering her presence.

"There is something new going on with the humans, Noethe", Star started to explain.

Noethe looked up at Star from his ledge, where he often overlooked the colony during the afternoon sun. "I hope that there has not been another dragon attack…."

"Oh no! That's not it at all…." Star Flower sat down on the ledge with him, playing with a flower stem as she spoke. "The humans have been speaking of something strange. We have overheard such happenings for some time, and the faeries will come to the assistance of these folk, as they are in need."

Sometimes, Noethe found himself becoming annoyed with Star. She took a long time to tell him her news, and he wondered if it was just he, or all of the dragons who felt this impatience. He said nothing.

"The humans have been in the realm for almost a millennium now, and their kind was never plentiful to begin with, yet they bore their offspring. What we heard from them is that some offspring are imperfect, and they have now

gathered them all together to banish them to another colony." Star paused, perhaps searching for the words to continue...

"They have mated too often within family lines. They don't follow the dragon rule of mating."

"I see" Said Noethe. Dragons were always cautious not to mate within their own family line. They knew this from the beginning of dragons, that the eggs would not hatch, or the dragons would not live, if hatchlings grew to mate each other. Dragons had the knowledge of their family line, and this did not occur within the dragon folk. Perhaps the humans did not know this, and the results were bad.

Star spoke again, "The humans had a gathering and took all of the folk that were imperfect or defective as they called them.
They sent them off into a glen far away, to fend for themselves. They were without hunting objects, and they cried so in hunger, that finally the faeries began to visit and teach them to gather food from the forest."

Noethe asked, "To what glen did the humans banish the imperfects? And do they have any chance of survival?"

"They do, Noethe." Star said. They are simple-minded, but they can learn to gather. We have made them amulets to protect them, and showed them the hollow trees where they can make homes. We have sent Rose, Hyacinth, Iris and Dianthus to watch over the "forest-folk". They lost some of their folk, when they were unable to distinguish edible plants, but now the faeries have taught them to gather and store food. They arrived in cast-off rough garments of the humans, not the animal skins that humans are fond of. The humans apparently did not want to kill their simple folk; they just wanted them away, banished to the warm region, in the valley."

Noethe contemplated this situation and decided to visit the forest folk with several trusted dragons, lead by Star Flower.

When Noethe arrived at the glen in the valley, he was accompanied by Gerethe from his own colony [since he always included a senior dragon and Noethe trusted him], as well as Kirethe from the north region, Hacethe from the west, and Bekethe from the east. Bekethe had assumed the leadership of the colony *of the east after Hanethe was killed by humans in the last millennium. Noethe himself was from the south region. Noethe loved the heat of the sun, and spent his leisure time basking on the ledge.*

Star Flower went ahead into the glen, and found her faerie sisters there, making ready the forest-folk, who were quite afraid of the dragons. Some tried to run, but Rose was able to calm them and show assurance that the dragons meant no harm.

The dragons looked the forest-folk over and decided that the faeries had done well to teach them, as they were surely simple in manner. How unfortunate that the humans gave birth to offspring, only to banish them to their own survival. Dragons would never send young or helpless to survive alone. Of course, they would not have mated in their own family line either and this seemed to be the dilemma of the humans now.

"Is there a forest-folk who will speak for the others? " Noethe asked.
Rose urged a young couple forward. Noethe thought them to be small but perhaps this was the nature of forest-folk. They did not speak readily, but when Rose whispered in the ear of the female, she finally uttered a few words. "I am Kathryn and this is Landis. Our people left us here, but Rose is helping us." She stepped back and looked at the ground.

Noethe spoke to Rose. "You have done well in your teaching, Rose." His own faerie-friend Star Flower whispered something in his ear. "Ah, yes. Star has suggested that the faeries give the forest-folk the means to call faeries to them, using firelight and herbs.

Kathryn seemed to be the one most forth-coming with speech, although Landis stayed at her side, showing support. "You will not harm us, great dragon?"

Noethe shook his massive head gently. "It is not in our nature to harm you, and we have the dragon code which we follow, preventing us from killing except in the hunt."
Rose spoke. "We have taught the forest-folk to gather. Here they have water, plants and shelter. The humans have cast them off, and offer neither protection nor support.
The faeries have taught them what they need to know, and will provide the herbs to prevent them from producing offspring. We will do what we can for them,

and we would not ask for dragon help, unless they are endangered in some way that faeries could not help them."

The meeting with forest-folk was ended, and Noethe took his leader dragons into another glen to speak freely. "Apparently these humans are an odd sort. They don't have codes to follow, and now they have banished their own. It surprises me that they have not killed the banished ones, but we do not understand the ways of humans enough. The faeries continue to provide us with information on humans. We will follow dragon code and keep unseen from humans as it is possible. It appears that their numbers have increased in this millennium, and they have human settlements in almost all of the regions, save the north. Be watchful of your colonies."

Ragethe finished scribing, and thought about the forest-folk. In his lifetime, their glen was occupied by perhaps the same number described by the lore of the past millennium, and true to their word, the faeries had provided the protection needed for the forest-folk not to produce offspring. The humans continued to banish more of them to the valley glen, but seemed unconcerned with their existence.

Ragethe thought of his own faerie-friend, Sunflower, in her pale yellow garment, who often brought him news of the realm, and marveled at the kind nature of faeries. He looked forward to his next meeting with Hycethe, and looked in wonder at his scribings, which now filled much of the great journal. Hycethe had been given the journal by his human friend Anslem, that they might record dragon lore.

Ragethe fell asleep in the early morning, grateful that Hycethe had set him to the task of scribing.

GARETHE

Chronicles of Dragon Lore V

Gerethe of the Third Millennium

Ragethe felt as if his scribing was endless, not that he would have complained. His scribing was a chronicle of many millennia of dragon lore, from the first millennium, recounting the earliest dragon memories, to the present time.

Moethe never minded the countless hours that Ragethe spent scribing. He spent time with her in the afternoon sun, and in the early evening hunt. Those were her favorite times of day. Ragethe chose the later hours of evening and into the night for his scribing, since it was quiet and Moethe usually slept.

Sunflower came to him at the end of the day to visit. She had nothing important to report, but Ragethe enjoyed her company. She was a bit different than other faeries, and perhaps that was the reason he was matched to Sunflower, as she was less-talkative than many of the others. "I am on my way to faerie feast this night, Ragethe. You may not see me for a day or two." She touched him gently on the ear and nose, showing her affection for the grey dragon. He nodded and she flew off into the evening.

This tale was told to me by Hycethe, the great dragon leader of the fourth millennium. He felt that he was more familiar with the third millennium, since his reign followed soon after. This was the time immediately prior to the terrible reign of Kenethe.

Gerethe had become Great Dragon Leader at the end of the second millennium, after the death of Noethe. Noethe was perhaps the longest reigning great dragon, living to over 800 years. His was a peaceful reign, as he held the dragon code close to him, taught by his predecessor and mentor Dracethe.

Gerethe became the pupil of Noethe, and as southern colony leader attended all of the meetings of the minds. The humans seemed to stay in their settlements, and dragons were safe for a time.

When Gerethe took over the southern colony, it was smaller than in times past. Some of the dragons had ventured across the blue sea and had not returned. Gerethe hoped that they had found new realms in which to live and hunt. Many dragons felt that with the existence of humans, the realm had become too small to provide enough prey for dragon and human. Gerethe saw no scarcity of prey in his lifetime. He took interest in the faeries, getting information on the forest-folk and humans from his faerie-friend, Buttercup.

Gerethe enjoyed a peaceful reign for most of the third millennium. Dragon-kind prospered, and Gerethe was a good leader. It was toward the latter part of the reign, that his faerie-friend Buttercup brought disturbing news to his ear.

She fluttered around Gerethe nervously, and told him "Do you recall many years ago, when a group of the southern dragons went over the blue sea?"

"Of course I do. That was many years past. What news do you carry?" Gerethe prompted Buttercup to continue.

"There have come a new group of dragons, with a leader called Kenethe. Faeries found that they are in the east, in the region of Bekethe and that they are sharing ideas with that colony, not within the thinking of dragons in your realm, great Gerethe."
Buttercup paused, "Violet, who is Bekethe's faerie-friend tells that he will not listen to the ideas of Kenethe, yet we sense trouble".

"What of the other colonies? The west colony of Hacethe and the north colony of Kirethe? Do they know of this dragon Kenethe?" Gerethe voiced his concerns to Buttercup, hoping that she had more news for him.

Buttercup shook her head. "I came to you first, Gerethe. We sent a faerie called Bluebell to Kenethe who will come to tell us of him. I do not know any more at this time."

Gerethe contemplated what Buttercup had told him and decided to travel to the east to meet with Kenethe and the other visiting dragons. He landed first in the eastern colony to see Bekethe, but was met on the outskirts by dragons of that colony that were fleeing. "Where are you going?" he asked of them.

One dragon who seemed to lead the group said he was Bekethe's son, Nomethe. "I am taking my mother and the others from here now. He has killed Bekethe. His body lies within the colony. Kenethe has named himself colony leader and says he is to meet with you..."

Angry, Gerethe scanned the area and located a group of dragons in an open field nearby. He did not think to be fearful of flying into the ranks of this new dragon, but landed amongst them. "I am Gerethe, Great Dragon Leader of the Realm. Which of you is Kenethe?"

The largest dragon of the group, black in color with vivid gold eyes answered Gerethe, "I am Kenethe, the new leader of this region. My warriors and I have come from the land over the blue sea, to seek new hunting grounds and to reside here."

Gerethe shook his head. "You apparently know nothing of our realm and dragon code. We do not challenge and seek to destroy our fellow dragons here. You would have been made welcome in this realm, as visitors. You had only to ask...."

"Ask? Kenethe said incredulously. "We ask for nothing. We take what we need and what we want. It is our way, the way of the land over the blue sea. We are warrior dragons, forced every day of our existence to defend our families and our hunting grounds from dragons and humans alike. We are used to doing battle to survive."

Gerethe tried to explain, "You might be descendents of a group of southern dragons who traveled over the blue sea many years ago. Perhaps the land there has different laws than we do. While you are in our realm, you will follow dragon code, which is not to attack or kill other dragons or humans. You may stay, if you abide by our code. What say you?"

Kenethe and his warrior dragons laughed. "You have no right to tell us what we may or may not do here. I have conquered this colony, which was my right. I am a warrior and I will attack whomever I please, dragon or human....." and with that, the entire group of warrior dragons attacked Gerethe, who thought *with his dying breath that he should have brought other dragons with him to meet with Kenethe, but now all was lost.....*

Ragethe paused after this story, since he knew first hand the evil and cruel nature of Kenethe. Kenethe had killed his own father, Banethe and the leader of his colony Rowethe. There was not another dragon in the realm that earned the fear and reigned with the terror that Kenethe demanded in the years to come.

So, it comes full circle, Ragethe thought. Even though I was born near the end of Kenethe's reign, at least I now know of his origins.

Such was the demise of the Great Dragon Gerethe, at the end of the third millennium. And so was chronicled the destruction that followed, under the reign of Kenethe.
In killing Gerethe, Kenethe proclaimed himself the new Great Dragon Leader, and none dared challenge him.

Kenethe and his warrior dragons took over the eastern colony, since the former residents had fled. The faerie Bluebell tried to befriend Kenethe, but he never trusted her, and sent her spying on other colonies and human settlements, only to use the information to attack them.

Humans soon became hostile to dragons, for the second time in dragon history there seemed to be a war between them. Kenethe was more interested in dragon rule than in attacking humans, but if he had the whim, the humans were not safe from the warrior dragons, who followed him without question.

The other colony leaders at the time were Kirethe in the north, Hacethe in the west and Rowethe in the south. These three leaders met regularly without the knowledge of Kenethe, but agreed that there was little to be done against this powerful dragon. Instead, they turned their attentions toward training their male dragons for battle, in case the need arose to defend their colonies. This was not something that fared well, since all of the older dragons believed in the dragon code, however, they saw no choice but to defend their families if it came to that. Everyone knew that, had Gerethe died a natural death, Rowethe would have been his successor. As a result, Kirethe and Hacethe followed Rowethe as their personally proclaimed leader, and at least in secrecy, did not advocate Kenethe and his disregard for dragon code.

Kenethe soon discovered the value of faeries and this was the time when he tricked his faerie, Bluebell into stealing magic from a human wizard with her music, and thereafter, administering the enchantments necessary to lure the humans into more battle.

Unfortunately, Kenethe had underestimated the vindictive behavior of humans, and they attacked his colony, killing his own mate and family. In his wrath, Kenethe sought to destroy any humans in his path.

My father, Banethe had been born in the eastern colony, descended from one of Kenethe's warrior dragons. He was raised and trained in the warrior tradition, but when he reached maturity and heard that Kenethe had deceived the faeries, devastating yet another human settlement, he left the colony. Luckily Banethe was already gone when the humans attacked.

Banethe sought out the western colony and Hacethe took him in. Banethe was accepted there, taking his mate, my mother Clarethe.

At this time Kenethe was outraged whenever dragons deserted his colony, especially male dragons that had been trained, and therefore, he felt, carried the secrets of battle that he guarded so well. His supporters were dwindling, and he often attacked former warrior dragons in their new colonies, or those in hiding. His frequent pastime was to crush the eggs of the ones he called traitors, and such was the fate of my mother's first laying.

This was when Kenethe wounded my father, and when my parents fled to a secret glen towards the south. My father dead, my mother raised my sisters and me, and the story converges to where we came to meet Rowethe in the southern colony.

Ragethe stopped scribing after this segment, most painful for him. This was the area in time when he had lost so much, and he sought to understand the events leading up to Kenethe's death. There had been no other way, and no dragon felt that Rowethe was wrong in putting an end to Kenethe and his destruction.

Perhaps the ways of the land over the blue sea were different than Dracethe's original dragon laws and code, but Kenethe had no right to abuse the realm and cause so much death.

Ragethe felt weary as he never had before when scribing. He was not fond of this time in dragon history, but Hycethe was right. The story had to be recounted, no matter how painful. In the future of dragon kind, it was important to chronicle all that had occurred, if only to avoid history repeating itself.

HYCETHE AND THE HUMAN PRINCE

The Chronicles of Dragon Lore VI

Hycethe and the Human Prince

Ragethe met with Hycethe this day, as he often did, but instead of hearing old dragon lore, the history of dragons, Hycethe regaled him of a recent encounter.

Hycethe lounged in the open field, in the afternoon sun, telling Ragethe of his meetings with Anslem, the human prince. Hycethe seemed pleased with the human encounters and still maintained hope that dragons could live in peace in the realm with humans.

The faeries, Sunflower and Hollyhock joined them for this meeting, and both dragons knew that they were fortunate in having the faeries as friends. They were helpful in communications, and that they lived so long as dragons meant having a longtime friendship.

When Ragethe returned to his chamber, he scribed the stories from that day....

Hycethe, in his previous meeting with the injured human, Anslem had learned of humans and their nature. Anslem, after his initial fear had dissipated decided that in the best interest of living together in the realm, it would be wise to continue this acquaintance with the great dragon Hycethe.

They met in the same field where Anslem was first injured, often staying for a number of hours or days, depending upon how much they both had to tell the other. Hycethe always went first, recounting recent dragon tales, happy to report that since the beginning of his reign, the attacks on humans had ceased. [He explained to Anslem of Kenethe and that his behavior was not typical for dragon kind]

Although humans took a long time to accept change, Anslem was their prince and the humans were receptive, for the most part in hearing of his meetings. Many asked to join them, but Anslem felt that meeting alone with Hycethe for now was best, until which time he could trust others to join him in this association.

Today, Hycethe had many questions.... "I have seen your objects for hunting, shiny but not made of rock. What manner of material are they?"

Anslem replied, "Our weapons are made of metals. We forge or heat them with fire and shape them into blades, with which to hunt. Other implements we shape for digging in the ground, planting, cutting trees, and building structures. As you can see, our hands are not suited to kill without weapons."

Hycethe nodded. "Metals... This is an unfamiliar word to me, but I understand the concept of it. Dragons have almost no possessions, and therefore humans are set apart in this way. You have garments, structures and weapons, yet you have families and hunt as dragons do."

Anslem said, "We are not so different in some ways, I think, great Hycethe. We both have intelligence; language, custom, and we both teach our young to survive. Our lifespan is not like a dragon. Oh, I wish I could look forward to a long life such as yours. I am considered middle-aged at 26 years old, and have children to raise that I may not see to adulthood. How gratifying it must be to see your grandchildren and great-grandchildren."

Hycethe shrugged. "It is natural for us. We do not question life as humans seem to. We live rather simply, it is true and our kind survive a great many years....I am 500 years old, middle-aged for a dragon, so perhaps we are of comparable age in our own species."

Anslem smiled. "It is amazing to me that I have met such a dragon as yourself, and have been given this opportunity to communicate. My people are interested in peace between us, and if you have gone forward with scribing your dragon history, it may be useful for me to have it copied for humans to learn, that our future human kind may understand dragon kind as I am starting to. We cannot hope for peace, if we have to be in fear of history repeating itself. I want no more battles with dragons."

"Yes, the scribing continues. Sometime I would like to you meet Ragethe, my scribe, as he is a most gentle dragon. I have told him of our meetings, and he scribes them regularly. He is working on the recording of our dragon history, which pleases him. He was born into a time of battles, having lost family, and he wishes peace as much as any dragon I have known." Hycethe wanted not to injure Anslem with his touch, so inched his limb close enough, hoping that Anslem would understand the gesture of friendship.

Anslem placed his hand on the cool dragon hide, marveling at its feel. "Be well, my dragon friend, and we shall meet again soon. Perhaps you should bring Ragethe, and I should choose one trusted human friend to bring as well." Anslem rose to his feet and bade Hycethe farewell for the day.

Ragethe thought of the prospect of meeting Anslem and decided that he would agree to accompany Hycethe to his next meeting. It would be interesting to see a human up close, and yet, more importantly, Ragethe felt that it would be a symbol of peace, this meeting of dragons and humans.

In a few days, Hycethe had set up a meeting with Anslem, sending his faerie-friend Hollyhock to Anslem, telling him that Ragethe would join them. It was the first time he had sent Hollyhock to a human, and she was apprehensive.
But, she had spied on Hycethe's last meeting with Anslem, and knew what he looked like. Hollyhock was able to see Anslem alone and he agreed to bring his brother with him to the meeting.

Hycethe and Ragethe arrived in the field, spotting Anslem and another human near the edge of the forest. As they approached, the humans came toward them. "Greetings Great Dragon Hycethe, this is my brother Aaron."

Hycethe bowed slightly and said, "Greetings to you Aaron. This is my friend Ragethe and he is also the dragon scribe who is chronicling our history."

"Aaron is also a scribe and I brought him in the hopes that he and Ragethe would find it interesting to exchange ideas." Anslem explained.

Ragethe nodded. "I am pleased to meet another scribe, Aaron. There is much pleasure for me in the recording of history. When Hycethe told me of human scribing, I felt that the task was somehow natural for me. I hope that sometime we will be able to share our journals."

Aaron said, "I wish you a great amount of luck, Ragethe, since my brother has told me that your task is to chronicle many millennia of dragon history. I am but one scribe in a series of scribes over time. One takes over for the previous one in each generation. I too enjoy my work, and am happy to meet with you anytime."

The meeting progressed with more stories of humans and dragons being exchanged, but mostly Hycethe and I were hopeful that with each meeting, we came closer to the time of peace that we only dreamed of in times past.

Aaron promised to bring some human records for Ragethe to read and Ragethe was very interested in this. There was still much that he felt they did not know about humans.

Ragethe decided to take on an apprentice scribe, since hearing that the task was passed on in human generations. Even though Ragethe had a longer life span and did not concern himself with death yet, he felt that a copy of his records should be scribed. He chose his own great-grandson Nobethe as apprentice, since he most reminded Ragethe of himself as a young dragon. He and Nobethe often spoke of such things for hours when his grandmother Clinethe was visiting Moethe.

Nobethe seemed intrigued with the idea of scribing, and promised to scribe the copy whenever he visited in the afternoons. In that respect, Ragethe could still do his own scribing in the evenings. Ragethe felt that he was passing on a valuable skill to his great-grandson, and it was something for the future dragons to look forward to, a dragon history, and the possibility of peace with the humans.

EVIL KENNETHE

The Chronicles of Dragon Lore VII
The Origins of the Evil Kenethe

Ragethe set out one evening to chronicle the story of Kenethe, as told to him by the grandson of Rennethe in Hycethe's presence not so long ago.

Rather uncertainly, the two year old Kenethe jumped off the embankment as his father urged him to fly. He was afraid, but could not admit this to his father, Agarthe who was a fierce dragon.

Kenethe, when around his father was complacent and obedient, as was demanded of him. When around other dragons of his age group, Kenethe was a bully, often antagonizing them into fighting. Numathe and Rennethe were his closest companions, and shared his aggression.

Years before, a group of elder dragons had fled the old realm, crossing the blue sea and had come to settle in a plains area at the base of a mountain range. The hunting was good in the beginning, the group small and well led by Rowgathe, proclaimed leader by the others.

Rowgathe was leader for almost a millennium, when he was killed by an accidental fall in a rock slide. He had landed on a ledge, overlooking the plains where the young dragons were hunting the horned beasts. He rose up to fly, when suddenly the ledge gave way, trapping a talon in the rocks. The rock slide caught Rowgathe in its path, pummeling him down the mountainside. By the time the young dragons reached their leader, he was dead.

Agarthe, who was the other adult dragon nearby looked into his dragon eye, setting his soul free. From that moment, Agarthe declared himself leader, not even waiting for the elders to convene or to discuss a successor.

Agarthe had always wanted to lead, but his cruel nature was known by Rowgathe, who had told him many times in the past that Dragons were passive creatures. Rowgathe had not named Agarthe as his successor, and felt he had time to consider a more worthy dragon.

Agarthe considered this passive nature a weakness in Rowgathe, and he dismissed the passive view, raising his own son Kenethe with harsh words and treatment, much to the dismay of his mate, Carbethe.

Kenethe emerged from the inconsistencies of his mother and father, a confused dragon, but took on the cruel nature of his father, Agarthe, as a matter of survival. It was not uncommon for Agarthe to strike either his mate or his son in anger, when they did not follow his wishes. As a result, Kenethe held his mother in high regard, but took on the ways of his father.

On the embankment, Agarthe roared at Kenethe. "Off with you, Kenethe! Let's see some speed in your take-off!" Kenethe did not hesitate, but took off in a low sweep down over the plain, then banking left, tore the throat out of the nearest beast.

"Good, good!" Agarthe nodded to his son with approval. Agarthe had not told the others, but he had been taking the young males on adventures, as he called them. He felt that they should learn battle and encouraged them to fight for a mate, often wounding each other. Upon returning from the adventures, Agarthe often spoke of "accidents" in his hunter training, which he used to account for the injuries. The fighting of other dragons was not something the elders would approve of, since they were passive.

Over time, Kenethe became a great battle dragon, not only making his father proud, but Kenethe realized that he was the strongest dragon in the plains. In his head, he planned the day when he might become leader, and plotted the demise of his father, Agarthe, whom he had come to hate.

Kenethe went off one day with some of his more loyal companions and landed near a cool pond to relax. He said casually, "Some of you know of my plan to become leader?" The dragons looked at each other, apprehensively. Numathe spoke first, since he was Kenethe's closest friend. "Kenethe, you know that we support you. We do not know the outcome of such a plot against Agarthe. What will the elders do, if we are found out?"

Kenethe laughed. "I am the strongest and fiercest. My father has trained us well. How do you suppose we will fail? As long as my plan takes us far enough from the plain, no dragon will know of the plot....that is, unless one of YOU speaks of it." He gestured threateningly towards the others.

Rennethe cried, "Kenethe, we would never betray you." He bowed toward Kenethe. "To our future leader!" Rennethe proclaimed. The others cheered, even though one or two of them were doing so out of fear, rather than loyalty.

Several days passed, and warm days were fading into cool days. Kenethe approached his father in the morning and spoke to him. "Great Leader Agarthe." He waited for a response, and when his father nodded, Kenethe continued. "Father, I wonder if we may venture further into the south today for our lessons? I have heard that the sun is warmer there, and that the hunting is good."

Agarthe saw no reason to deny Kenethe this request. He tired of the same hunting grounds as much as any of them. "We shall venture south, then."

Flying for some time south of the plains, Agarthe finally landed in a wooded area inside a clearing. "Good choice, my son. Let us seek the prey here, and determine what beasts dwell in the wood. Come, I hunger for the hunt." And Agarthe took off.

Kenethe signaled to the others, and taking off, they sprung against Agarthe from the rear, swooping and clawing at him in the air, until he was grounded. No mercy was shown to their leader, for he must not survive such an attack. Rennethe finally examined the lifeless Agarthe and declared him slain. A cheer rose from the throat of Kenethe. "I am leader!" The others bowed before him. One dragon, Rogethe did not share their enthusiasm, but would not dare to challenge Kenethe.

All afternoon, they planned their story. They would return to the plain without Agarthe, and could not take the chance of repeating inconsistent tales to the elders. Kenethe spoke. "It's settled then. We were unfamiliar with the wood, when suddenly a pack of huge, clawed beasts fell upon my father, who was reclining in the sun. They attacked well and quickly, and since we were in flight, not close enough to assist Agarthe, he was killed by them. We, of course, vanquished the clawed beasts and devoured them." He nodded, as if he felt that his story was free from suspicion.

After disposing of Agarthe's remains in the wood, so they could not be seen from the air, Kenethe and his band returned to the plain at nightfall. Sounding the alert, they recounted the horrific tale of the attack on Agarthe. The elders looked at each other. They had been settled in the plains area for much time, and it was true that they had not ventured as far south as Agarthe had lead the youths that day.

Kenethe proclaimed. "I am leader now! My father wished it for me with his last breath. I have looked into his dragon eye and set free his soul! Who would challenge me as leader?" He looked around.

The elders knew of the cruelty of Agarthe, and of his son Kenethe. Kenethe's own mother, Carbethe spoke. "My son, take me to Agarthe. I must see for myself that he is dead." The elders looked to Kenethe for his reply.

"Alas, mother, I cannot." Kenethe glanced at Numathe and Rennethe to corroborate his story. "The clawed beasts did extreme damage, and even as we watched, the scavengers set upon his poor carcass. I fear there is nothing left to see, mother….and I cannot bring myself to re-enter the southern wood, for fear that the clawed beasts would attack you or me."

Carbethe nodded sadly. Agarthe had not treated her well, but she did not wish him dead. Other dragons murmured to themselves, until Kenethe spoke again. "I declare the southern wood off-limits, until the most experienced hunters deem it safe to approach. I will lead a hunting party after a time."

Many days passed, and Rennethe came to Kenethe, who was relaxing in the sun, feeling very smug and proud of becoming leader. "Kenethe, I must tell you something I heard from my sister Jannethe." Kenethe nodded. "You know that she is mate to Rogethe, who was with us in the wood….."

Kenethe said. "Out with it, if you have something to say" He was impatient with his friend, but a spark of uncertainty fell over him as he urged Rennethe to continue.

"I overheard Jannethe speaking to my mother. She said things about the hunt that she could only have heard from Rogethe, since I do not speak of them… Then I heard whispers of a plot against Agarthe and…"

"WHAT?" Kenethe roared and rose up, striking Rennethe. "What has he done? We swore silence, and you all swore loyalty to ME." Kenethe's eyes were wild with anger. Rennethe backed up so that Kenethe would not further strike him.

"We shall see about this...." Kenethe said, and gestured for Rennethe to follow him.

They saw the elders in the meeting circle, with Rogethe and Jannethe in the middle, speaking quietly. As Kenethe approached, the eldest dragon Marnethe spoke solemnly to the group, but directed his words to Kenethe. "It is with great sorrow that I have heard the actual events that took place in the southern wood. What dragon would plot to destroy his own father, the leader?" Marnethe shook his head. "I am an old dragon and do not want to lead, but Kenethe, you have betrayed us. The elders have decided that I am to be leader..."

Kenethe interrupted. "You cannot do this! I AM LEADER!" The other dragons stirred around him, and Kenethe was unaware of the positioning of the male elders surrounding him in a loose circle, as his anger overwhelmed his sense of reason.

Marnethe spoke again. "No, Kenethe. I am leader. You have done a great misdeed, for which you and your loyal following will be banished from our colony, never to return again. We will not allow plotting and killing of our own kind. Be gone, NOW!" And the elders started pushing against Kenethe, Rennethe, Numathe and the other loyals, until they were outside the circle. The remainder of the dragons stood behind Marnethe in support. Marnethe repeated. "Be gone."

Kenethe and the others had no choice but to leave. They flew in silence until they reached the southern wood, where their deeds had brought this upon them. Numathe spoke first. "Where shall we go?" Rennethe and the others looked at Kenethe for leadership. "You will always be leader to me. We shall follow you." The loyal dragons bowed to Kenethe.

"Perhaps all is not lost." Kenethe said thoughtfully. "Our elders came from across the blue sea. We have heard the lore of our past there. We shall fly long and hard across the blue sea and forge our own colony there. Come, my friends." And they flew outward toward the blue sea, following Kenethe into the unknown.

Ragethe paused. He could understand the events that produced a dragon of such evil outlook, such as Kenethe. I did not feel empathy for him, since Kenethe had been responsible for so many deaths, but it was helpful to know this tale. Ragethe was grateful for this, as well as all of the dragon-lore collected in his Chronicles, if only to prevent such evil from occurring again.

FAERIE QUEEN

Chronicles of Dragon Lore VIII

The Nature of Faeries

One late afternoon, Ragethe was speaking to his faerie-friend Sunflower. She was enjoying a cup of fresh milk, as Ragethe and she chatted on the ledge outside of his chamber. Ragethe could hear Moethe singing to herself inside while lighting the fire for the evening.

Ragethe was telling Sunflower about the humans, and his scribings of dragon lore, when suddenly it dawned on him that he had written nothing about faeries.
"How would it be for you to give me your faerie history, that I might scribe the faerie chronicles?"

Sunflower didn't really understand scribing or chronicles, but she saw this as an opportunity to tell stories, which was something she loved to do. "Shall I provide more stories to you, Ragethe? I think that my mistress, Queen Anne's Lace would like to know of this. I would ask her if I may bring you to a faerie feast, that you might hear faerie stories and singing." And suddenly, she was gone, apparently off to see the queen faerie.

I had never heard of the faerie Queen Anne's Lace, nor had he heard any dragon mention her, but he was very intrigued by such an idea. Ragethe was an experiential dragon, loving new stories to scribe, and now that he had met forest-folk and humans, why shouldn't he meet the faerie queen too?

Sunflower returned the next night to tell Ragethe of the upcoming faerie feast. "You may bring fresh milk to our Queen as a gift, if you like" and Ragethe nodded.

My experience with the faerie-feast was nothing like I had ever seen the likes of before in my days. When Sunflower led me into the faerie-glen, the night was ablaze with firelight and music. Dragons were relatively quiet beings, without such merry-making and I was interested to meet the faerie queen and to hear their stories.

In the clearing, the shape of a great ring appeared to me, all lined with faeries. Many I knew as the faerie-friends to dragon leaders, as Sunflower was to me. I longed to ask many questions and hoped that I would have the opportunity.

Just ahead of me, at the head of the circle, there sat most beautiful creature I had even seen. She had very long dark hair, flowing out and curling in all directions. Her eyes were large, expressive and painted to emphasize them. She saw me immediately and nodded her greeting. I bowed slightly to her in reverence to her position. Her garment was a flowing pure white gown of what seemed like transparent silk, decorated with many tiny objects causing it to glitter in the firelight. Her feet were bare, as were the feet of all of the faeries.

I glanced around the circle, and realized how few of the faeries I might actually have met. I saw Tulip, Gardenia, and Dahlia, friends of the leaders, and Hollyhock, who was friend to the Great Dragon Leader Hycethe. I also saw the forest faeries, Rose, Iris, Hyacinth and Dianthus. The faeries wore many different colored garments, but not to be confused with the queen, theirs were not as long or ornate. All of the lesser faeries had long hair, but only the queen's hair was the dark ebony color.

Not knowing how to conduct myself, I waited for invitation or instructions. As if on cue, two unknowns, on either side urged me forward into the center of the ring to address the queen. I laid my offering of goat's milk down before her and she nodded her thanks.

I stood before her, and she spoke in a voice that dripped like the morning dew, mesmerizing me as I gazed at her eyes. "Dragon Ragethe, be welcome at our faerie-feast. I am known as Queen Anne's Lace. We have sat in wonder, that no dragon has visited us in times past, but let us not dwell on this. I have welcomed news of the realm from the faeries all through the millennia, and some of it has been dragon-lore. You are the first dragon that has been here. We will start the faerie-feast now. Feel free to participate or watch from the edge of the ring, since the faeries will dance here."

I stepped back to the opposite side and settled down to watch the faeries. There was much music, singing and dancing for quite some time. To the side, there were feasts laid out of milk, honey, berries and other morsels known to faeries. This was a joyous event and the faeries seemed ecstatic in their dancing...a different sort of view of faeries than what I had witnessed with faeries as dragon friends and communicators.

When the dancing was finished, all of the faeries enjoyed the delicacies of their feast. Many faeries spoke to me, and were happy that I had come to visit. Sunflower came to me and whispered into my ear, as was her way. "Ragethe, you may now have audience with the queen and ask your questions of her"

The other faeries left us to our conversation, save two that were apparently in attendance to the queen. "Greetings, Queen Anne's Lace of the faeries. I know not what to ask, but I will tell you that I am the appointed scribe of dragon-lore, assigned to this task by the Great Dragon Leader Hycethe. I have many questions and hope to learn of faerie-folk and culture. Faeries have been in the realm for as long as the dragons, and yet we know little of you."

The Queen smiled. "Faeries have indeed been in the realm a long time and perhaps longer than dragons. We came overland from another realm and made our home here many millennia ago. We recall the arrival of dragons from over the blue sea. We befriended dragons immediately, as we are social creatures. My faeries love the dragon-friends, and I always send a faerie to each new dragon leader. It is a sad day for the faerie whose dragon-friend is gone in death, as she must return to me then."

I asked "Are these faeries never sent to a second dragon, after the death of a dragon-friend?"

"No, Ragethe. It is such a close companionship, the faerie to the dragon, that the faerie would never again be happy. Many faeries remain here in service to their queen, and this is our custom. I send a faerie to a dragon, both to establish the friendship and to provide communication within the realm. As you know, all of our communications are verbal. Faeries have no written language. I have also sent four faeries, to the forest-folk, as they are in need. You know them as Rose, Iris, Hyacinth and Dianthus. I will not send faeries to humans, as I find them to be barbaric in nature. We will listen to the humans, as has been done since their arrival."

I was intrigued. "Are there male faeries or only females as I see represented here?"

"Faeries are capable of assuming either gender, but it pleases me to have the faeries as they are around me. If we require reproduction, once each millennium, I will instruct the mating and males would be in appearance." The Queen was very patient with my questions, and I was uncertain whether anyone had asked of faerie nature before my visit.

I asked another question. "What of faerie amulets?"

Queen Anne replied. "The amulet is wrought with faerie magic. It contains the essence of the flower of each faerie name, along with protective herbs and scents which are the very nature of our being. Each faerie wears an amulet, and we are not aware that other beings have this custom, although I did instruct the forest faeries to devise amulets for the forest-folk. They are so fragile it is uncertain whether the amulet will provide much protection to them. Part of the amulet that I have not yet mentioned is dragon's blood. In the case of a slain dragon, we visit the site and collect dried dragon's blood. Did you know that the Dracaena Draco tree evolved from dragon's blood?"

I shook my head. "What is the meaning of the tree?"

She responded and held an amulet before her. "The tree contains sap derived from the blood of slain dragons. The sap hardens into resin and it has added strength to our amulets. I have a gift for your mate. Give this amulet to Moethe as it contains the blood of your son Darethe. She need not wear the amulet, as I know it is not the way of dragons, but please have her keep it close to her, and tell her that his blood has nourished many amulets. Although a death of a dragon is a great loss, the spirit of the dragon will be remembered, and the strength of the dragon is present for all eternity in the Dracaena Draco tree, which did not appear until the first dragon died in the realm. We knew it was of great significance."

I accepted her gift, and was deeply moved by her words, for Darethe was my lost son, as well as the son of Moethe. He was slain in the battle with Kenethe in the last millennium, a time best forgotten. I thanked the Queen for her generosity.

I left the faerie glen and went back to my ledge and my journal, knowing that I, Ragethe had just forged a new segment in history. It was the faeries who had made the effort to become friends to dragons, and I felt that a great injustice had been done to them, by our accidental lack of interest in faerie-folk.
I vowed to speak to Hycethe on this, and was of the hope that he would sometime return with me to a faerie-feast.

I brought the faerie amulet to Moethe. I was uncertain whether she would accept the gift easily, since Darethe's death seemed to weigh heavily upon her, even though so much time had passed.

"Dear Ragethe. I will accept the amulet from the faerie queen. I feel that she somehow spoke to me in a dream sometime ago, when I was told of the Dracaena Draco tree and dragon's blood. How would I have known of it, otherwise? It was a thoughtful gesture and I will keep it with me, as the queen intended. I believe that the faeries may be helpful in the quest for peace that you and Hycethe so long for. They are a magical being, with properties we do not understand. I will dream of my poor Darethe tonight....."

I touched Moethe gently as she passed into our chamber, and was grateful that I had visited the faerie feast tonight.

HYCETHE SPEAKS OF PEACE

Chronicles of Dragon Lore IX

Hycethe and the Realm of Peace

Ragethe looked at the journal he often referred to as the Chronicles of Dragon Lore. In reading all of the scribings that he had worked on for many years. He recalled meetings that he had attended with Hycethe and the humans. Ragethe felt that Anslem and Aaron had become his friends, and through his association with Aaron, Ragethe had learned a great deal about humans.

He no longer felt that humans were barbarians, as the faeries had suggested. They had intelligence; however, Ragethe believed it was the human's vulnerability and short life that made them so different in their customs.
It was difficult to be a dragon that might live 1000 years, and imagine living less than 100 years as a human. Still, Ragethe found the humans interesting to learn about, and through Aaron's human scribings, there was much history.

Moethe entered the chamber and spoke to Ragethe. "Are you still scribing, Dear Ragethe?"

"No, I am reading the journal section on humans." Ragethe said. He sometimes read to Moethe from the journal, that she might understand the nature of humans, and the dragon lore.

In the time when humans first came to the realm, they were afraid. The trip they made over the blue sea was wrought with hardship and their losses were great. They endured the heavy task of building their shelters, and had they arrived later, they may not have survived the winter months.

Humans chose the middle region to settle in, being furthest from the blue sea that they had come to despise from their voyage. The region had plentiful stone and timber for building and fires, and had good hunting.
They were fond of the game birds and the herds of beasts that roamed the fields. Their numbers were few at first, perhaps 40 in number, but within a few years, their numbers had tripled.

The humans felt that they had chosen well in the realm. The discovery of dragons was sorely distressing to them. The death of one of their own by a dragon initiated the subsequent attacks on the dragon colonies, and this went on for millennia, until the meetings with Hycethe and Prince Anslem commenced.

The humans were skeptical, if not hopeful that there might be peace between dragons and humans. They left the negotiations in the hand of Anslem, while keeping in readiness, if it became necessary to defend or attack the dragons again. Theirs was a society with a leader, and Anslem was the authority, such as the dragons had the Great Dragon Leader. In this respect, the dragons felt optimistic, since the meetings with Anslem and Hycethe went well.

This recounting of a brief portion of human history cannot replace their own history, and I note that Aaron provided me with a copy of their scribed human history, since the time they arrived in the realm.

Ragethe looked into the segment in which he had described the forest-folk, and much later, the conversation that he and Hycethe had with Anslem regarding these unfortunate folk.

In a meeting with Hycethe and the human Prince Anslem, I learned about the forest-folk, from the humans. Hycethe had always been curious about them, ever since the faeries took us to meet Kathryn and Landis, years before.

Hycethe asked "Prince Anslem, I wonder about the humans that we call the forest-folk. Would you tell me of them?"

Anslem looked somewhat embarrassed and told us, "If you refer to the unfortunate humans of the glen, then I can tell you of them. In our previous land, any child born or young adult that was discovered to be defective in physical traits or damaged in thinking was put to death. Somehow, my ancestors thought that humans would not give birth to these persons once we left our land across the blue sea. It was a land of disease and of violence. Did you know that there are also dragons there?"

Ragethe and Hycethe exchanged a knowing glance and nodded, thinking that this was where Kenethe and his band of warrior dragons had come from

Anslem continued, "The births of unfortunate ones did not stop in this land, and finally the physicians and wizards told us that we were causing or increasing the imperfections, by not keeping track of parentage and family lines. We have since remedied our record keeping, and hope that the unfortunate ones are less in number."

"Why do you not keep them with you, if they are your own?" Hycethe inquired of Anslem.

Anslem replied. "If you knew of the land we arrived from, the elders were adamant about putting the unfortunates to death. A small group of my ancestors, horrified by this practice, one time instead took them to the glen, showing them food, and giving them what they thought of as a chance at survival. In later times, it was apparent that they had learned to forage and survive on their own."
"They had not reproduced, and the ones that were occasionally added to the original group became less and less over time. It is our hope that it becomes no longer necessary to banish them, that we can correct our failures and learn to teach even the unfortunates. None have been banished since the start of my reign"

Hycethe responded. "I have met some of the forest-folk. In the beginning, there were Kathryn and Landis that seemed as the leaders, but they have passed into death some years ago." Then Hycethe asked, "Do you know of faeries?"

Anslem nodded. "Faeries have made themselves known to me on occasion, although I cannot tell you when I have seen one recently."

Hycethe motioned to Hollyhock, who he knew to be lurking nearby. She flew in and settled down next to him. "This is Hollyhock, my faerie-friend. I can tell you that the reason that your forest-folk survived at all was due to the kindness of her faerie-sisters. They taught your folk to gather food and shelter themselves."

Anslem looked at Hollyhock. "Then I thank you and your faerie-folk for looking after our unfortunates, Hollyhock."

Moethe spoke to Ragethe. "Dear Ragethe, I was thinking of the hunt." Ragethe smiled and went off to hunt with his Moethe. He could refuse her nothing, as she was his joy.

Later in the night, when Ragethe came back to his scribing, he paused to think about how he and his great-grandson Nobethe had spent hours together, with him training Nobethe to scribe a copy of the chronicles. When it was completed, Ragethe presented the copy to Aaron, the human scribe. He saw the age in Aaron's face and wondered about the length of his life.

He, Ragethe would continue for many years past when Aaron would be gone in death. He wanted very much to share their chronicles before that time occurred. Aaron brought Ragethe the human history at the same time, and their friendship, initiated by the meetings with Hycethe and Anslem now seemed sealed, with their mutual histories in hand. He recounted the day....

I looked over the volumes of the human history, anxious to read them. "Ragethe, I have brought you not only what I have scribed myself, but also what was scribed before my time, as far back as our arrival from over the blue sea." Aaron accepted the copy I gave him of our chronicles. "I will treasure this, and will share the dragon-lore at our fires, in the hope that knowing of this will help us make peace."

I nodded at Aaron, wondered how such a gentle human could exist amongst the violent ones who attacked dragons. But, as it was with dragons, I realized we were the same. I was considered a peaceful and contemplative dragon, especially when compared to battle dragons of my past. It was true that I had trained and fought in battle, but it was in my nature to remain alone with my Moethe and scribe the dragon-lore.

"My uncle, the brother of my father was the scribe who taught me. He was but one of many scribes of our history, recording births, deaths and events of the years. When I have read the long-past history of the times when we seemed to be at war with dragons, I felt sorrow. My ancestors left the land over the blue sea to escape from war. I feel lucky that my life has not been filled with these hard

times. I thank you for your chronicles. I will treasure them, Ragethe". Aaron
stood and bowed to me as he departed.
We always met in the same field, and even though I often thought of taking
him to see Moethe, I chose not to do this, since I would not want to endanger
my Moethe, if something went wrong. My dwelling with Moethe was, after all,
hidden.

One day Sunflower, my faerie-friend appeared to me, beckoning me to a
dragon meeting of the minds. I took off immediately, meeting Hycethe and
the colony leaders in the meeting glen in the southern region. Hycethe had
for some time included me in these meetings, since I would scribe them,
and no colony leader objected to my presence.

I looked upon the dragon Nomethe of the east, son of the slain Bekethe,
who had returned to his colony after the death of Kenethe. His faerie,
Pansy hovered near his head.

I then saw Dogethe of the western colony, with the faerie Dahlia. I noticed
the advanced age of Dogethe and remembered that his predecessor Hacethe
had lived past 1000 years. Perhaps the climate of the west agreed with
dragons.

Kolethe of the north was present, with the faerie Juniper, dressed in a
dark green garment. I knew the least of the north region, being fond of
the warmer climates.

And finally, the southern colony leader Bagethe was there with the faerie
Honeysuckle. Bagethe was the successor of Hycethe for colony leader,
when Hycethe became Great Dragon Leader. Bagethe was also grandson
of Rowethe and had his bronze coloring, bringing me back to memories
of my time in their colony with my mother and sisters.

The dragons all settled down for the meeting, waiting for Hycethe to speak.
I remembered and returned to my chamber later to scribe the meeting.

Hycethe said, "Colony leaders, I have called this meeting to give you news. As
you know, Ragethe the scribe and I have met for many years now with the
human Prince Anslem, and also with his scribe Aaron. Ragethe now has in
his possession a history of the humans, scribed by them. He has supplied a

chronicle of dragon-lore and history to the humans, so that they might know of our kind."

Hycethe looked at the leaders. "As you know, we have seen too much death. Some regions have had terrible loss, especially the eastern and southern colonies. We will remember our lost leaders today.

There were some dragon leaders who lived to old age with dignity, such as the Great Dracethe and Noethe of the south, Kirethe of the north and Hacethe of the west."

"I never again want to hear of the death of dragons by human hand, as in the case of poor Hanethe of the east. Other dragons slain by humans during that time are mourned as well."

"I am saddened with the memory of the slaughter of our other leaders, due to the cruelty of the evil dragon Kenethe who invaded from the land over the blue sea nor do I desire to hear of the blatant disregard for dragon-code, founded by our Great Leader Dracethe.

The killing of Bekethe, Gerethe and Rowethe of the south and Banethe of the east by Kenethe is a part of dragon history that I wish we did not have to include in our chronicles.

For the sake of all future dragons, I beseech all of you leaders. Come with me now to a meeting with the human Prince Anslem, and forge the peace that we have so longed for." Hycethe finished and looked again to his colony leaders. "What say you all?"

Nomethe spoke first. "My father Bekethe was slaughtered by Kenethe. I fled the colony with my family until Kenethe was destroyed. I vow to forge peace with the humans and to upkeep the dragon code."

Bagethe said, "I have been in the south, through a time of battles and the death of my grandfather, to the region now being one of peaceful times. I agree."

Dogethe and Kolethe both added their agreement to their fellow leaders and Hycethe spoke once more. "Then join me in flight, colony leaders, and Ragethe the scribe. Make dragon history this day. Let us venture forth and let there be peace with the humans."

It was quite a sight, four colony leaders, each large in their own right. Nomethe, the gold; Bagethe, the bronze; Dogethe and Kolethe the black dragons, and the Great Gold Dragon Hycethe at the head of the group. I stayed to the rear, I, Ragethe the grey. I was not a leader, and I also was in awe of the view before me. I would have the task of scribing this meeting, this flight and this day before us.

It was hence that Hycethe, the four colony leaders and I landed on the field to meet with the human Prince Anslem. He had brought with him his scribe and my friend Aaron, who nodded and bowed to me. In addition, there were many other humans with Anslem, a delegation of various males and females, who pointed and looked at us with both fear and curiosity.

Anslem spoke first in this fateful meeting. "My people, and dragon-folk, this is a great and wonderful day. We have come here to proclaim peace between us. Those dragons and those human- folk here in this place will witness this proclamation for all others not present today. As Prince of the settlement of the new realm, I vow that no war will be made against the dragon-folk and shall it be scribed so by Aaron." The humans murmured and nodded their approval.

Hycethe rose up to his full height, a magnificent dragon for all to see. "My good humans, and dragon leaders, I am humbled before you. I show you my great size, but vow to you here that I seek peace between humans and dragons. I give my word in this matter and I speak for all of the dragons. The vow of peace shall be scribed by Ragethe."

This was perhaps the greatest segment of dragon-lore that I had ever scribed. From the time of hiding after my father's death to the day of the great meeting with the humans, I had hoped for peace.

I left my scribing to join my Moethe in our chamber, certain that I would sleep the free slumber of the dragon inside me who had realized yet one of my life's dreams.......

AARON THE HUMAN SCRIBE

Dragon Lore

At the first hint of twilight
After each day's hunt
Ragethe settles in to scribe

Long into night
Pouring over his quill
Writing as if to survive

Nature of faeries
Dark dragon past
Ragethe recalls the lore

Human destruction
To the realm of peace
Stories to be explored

Dracethe and Noethe
Great Dragon Leaders
Penned for all to read

Remembered sons
Forgotten evil
Lessons all must heed

Years in passing
Human friends
Messages to send

Hycethe's dream
Peace in the realm
And so his scribing ends

For now....

Written by Julie A. Dickson
Illustrations by Robin A. Morini
Poems: The Invitation, Dragon Love, Moethe's Faerie Dream by Robin A. Morini
Poem: Dragon Lore by Julie A. Dickson

MOETHE

About the Author:

Julie A. Dickson has been writing poetry and stories throughout her life. She is an avid animal lover, especially cats and dragons. She makes her home in New Hampshire.

Ms. Dickson is the author of Forest Nectars: A Collection of Poetry and two children's picture books.

Also published by Trafford:
- *Caterpillar*
- *Fat Cat Buys a Hat*

DRACETHE

About the Illustrator:

Robin A. Morini is an artist and lover of dragons and all things mystical.